# The Night Shift Before Christmas

by Isaac Gómez

SAMUEL FRENCH

**FOR PRODUCTION INQUIRIES**

UNITED STATES AND CANADA
info@concordtheatricals.com
1-866-979-0447

UNITED KINGDOM AND EUROPE
licensing@concordtheatricals.co.uk
020-7054-7298

Each title is subject to availability from Concord Theatricals Corp., depending upon country of performance. Please be aware that *THE NIGHT SHIFT BEFORE CHRISTMAS* may not be licensed by Concord Theatricals Corp. in your territory. Professional and amateur producers should contact the nearest Concord Theatricals Corp. office or licensing partner to verify availability.

## MUSIC AND THIRD-PARTY MATERIALS USE NOTE



## IMPORTANT BILLING AND CREDIT REQUIREMENTS

*THE NIGHT SHIFT BEFORE CHRISTMAS* was commissioned and developed by the Alley Theatre (Rob Melrose, Artistic Director; Dean R. Gladden, Managing Director) in Houston, Texas, with dramaturgical support from Elizabeth Frankel. The play received its world premiere at the Alley Theatre on December 8, 2024. It was directed by KJ Sanchez, with dramaturgy by Bradley Michalakis, scenic and lighting design by Kevin Rigdon, costume design by David Arevalo, sound design by Kathy Ruvuna, music direction by Jack Beetle, and voice and dialect coaching by Micha Espinosa. The production stage manager was Kaylee Sarton McCray. The cast was as follows:

**MARGOT** . . . . . . . . . . . . . . . . . . . . . . . . . . . . . . . . . . . . . . . . . Briana J. Resa

**VOICES** . . . . . . . . . . . . . . . . . . . . . . . . . . . . . . . . . . . . . . . . Orlando Arriaga

**MARGOT UNDERSTUDY** . . . . . . . . . . . . . . . . . . . . . . . . . . . . Elissa Cuellar

# CHARACTERS

**MARGOT** – A Scrooge. Born Margarita Adelina Maydenita Chihuahuita Adelante Sabado Gigante Muñoz. But that's only for family. To everyone else, she goes by Margot.

When possessed by spirits, she also plays:

**JACKIE** – a Jacob Marley, of sorts

**CLYDE** – in the realm of Christmas Past

**RICO** – in the realm of Christmas Lost; a Tiny Tim left behind

**GRACIE** – in the realm of Christmas Present

**DOLORES** – a warning akin to a Christmas Yet to Come

The voices of **ROBOTIC SANTA**, **BOOMING VOICE**, **RAÚL**, and **CUSTOMER** should be prerecorded and incorporated as part of the sound design.

**MARGOT** should be our sole live actor onstage.

# SETTING

Happy Burger.

A small but mighty family-owned, local fast food burger joint in Houston, Texas.

Though it could honestly feel like any local family-owned fast food joint anywhere in these here United States.

A warm and happy place.

# TIME

Present day.
Just before midnight.
Christmas Eve.

# AUTHOR'S NOTES

**A Note on Casting**
The actor playing Margot should identify as Latina. All identities within the Latina diaspora are welcome, with priority consideration for Black, Brown, and Indigenous Latinas.

**A Note on Music**
"Away in a Manger" and "Noche de Paz" are performed a cappella using traditional melodies and lyrics. Both songs are in the public domain.

"Christmas, Just Like" is an original song written and composed by Isaac Gómez, with arrangements by Jack Beetle. A lead sheet will be delivered digitally upon approval of a performance license.

**A Note from the Playwright**
This is a play about people who work on or around Christmas – people who find magic in the mundane, comedy in the tragic, and light in the dark. It's a play about a woman who chooses to be lonely even though she isn't alone, and her journey to discovering why that is, what she's avoiding, and what might be the alternative.

This is a play about Texas. And family-owned fast food joints. And the holidays. And so many collisions of life, love, heartbreak, joy, messiness – and everything the crevices of the human existence can't quite contain. It's at once hilarious as it is scary as it is sad, and everything in between. Lean into the moments of tone shifts. The audience will hunger for them.

Oh – and the possessions in this play? They're less *The Exorcist* and more *Scary Movie* franchise. It's so scary it's funny. Or so funny it's terrifying.

Lastly, push against sentimentality at all costs. Until it's earned.

For Liz Frankel.
Who always plans ahead.

And for Dolores.
Wherever I go...you won't be too far.

*"Do any human beings ever realize life while they live it – every, every minute?"*

**– Emily, *Our Town* by Thornton Wilder**

*"It was always said of him, that he knew how to keep Christmas well, if any man alive possessed the knowledge."*

**– *A Christmas Carol* by Charles Dickens**

*(The inside of a Texas-bred and beloved, blessed and highly favored, mom-and-pop, family-owned burger bar in Houston, Texas. Across the street is a Catholic Church, next door is a family home from the 1940s, and behind is a crematorium. Near midnight.)*

*(Christmas decorations are scattered throughout the restaurant. A small, sad, little Christmas tree with several Texas-themed ornaments stands proudly by the register counter. There's also a sad blue cardigan, hanging on the back of a plastic chair, seemingly unimportant until it is.)*

*(Light Christmas music plays from the radio overhead [something like Mariah Carey's "Christmas, Baby Please Come Home"].* A small "ding" is heard as a car pulls up to the drive-thru window.)*

*(Beat. A moment. Then –)*

*(A pre-recorded voice is heard from just outside the drive-thru window – something that automatically plays whenever a car pulls up.)*

---

**RAÚL**. *(Voice-over. <u>Too</u> cheerful.)* Howdy! Hola! Bonjour! Welcome to Happy Burger! This is Raúl speaking, founder and President of Joy, bringing you Crispy Cheer with every bite since 1979. Hang tight – someone will be with you shortly. Ciao!

> *(The sound of a car humming, waiting impatiently can be heard. A moment. Then –)*
>
> *(The car outside honks once.)*
>
> *(Nothing.)*
>
> *(Then, it honks again.)*
>
> *(Nothing.)*
>
> *(Then, it honks and it honks and it honks and it honks –)*

**MARGOT**. *(Offstage; running in.)* I'm comin', I'm comin'!

> *(**MARGOT** bursts in from the back room – drenched in sweat – carrying three stacks of large cardboard boxes labelled, "Secret Happy Sauce" It's heavy.)*

*(Mumbling; to herself.)* Everyone always wants somethin' from me, sheesh.

> *(Honk, honk, honk, honk –)*

I said I'm comin'!

> *(**MARGOT** swings the boxes around the counter to place them down but knocks over the small Christmas tree in the process; a few plastic ornaments come crashing down with it, scattering everywhere.)*

*(More than peeved.)* Of course. Story of my stupid life.

*(The car keeps honking. She'll deal with the mess later.)*

*(**MARGOT** walks over to a wall with a headset, puts it on, clears her throat.)*

*(Into the headset; not Happy.)* Welcome to Happy Burger, proud home of the Happy Burger, where the burgers are hot and the holiday spirit is Happy-sized. Would you like to try our Merry & Bright Happy Burger Combo today? It comes with a side of cheer.

*(Mumbling heard from the headset à la Charlie Brown's teacher.)*

*(Into the headset.)* No, okay.

So what can I get you.

*(More mumbling.)*

*(Into the headset.)* Uh huh.

*(More mumbling.)*

*(**MARGOT** looks over into the kitchen.)*

*(Into the headset.)* It'll be five minutes for the Onion Thrills, that okay with you?

*(Beat. A moment. She peeks into the kitchen again. More mumbling.)*

*(Into the headset.)* No Texas Twirls tonight but we *do* have Family Frites. You want those?

*(More mumbling.)*

*(Into the headset; typing into the register.)* Okay.

Okay.

Okay...

So. That'll be a Jalapeño with Cheese Happy Burger, Happy-sized with a Dr. Pepper, also Happy-sized. And a Double Happy Smiley Melt, also Happy-sized with a Happy-sized Coke.

*(Mumbling from the other side.)*

*(Into the headset.)* Coke <u>*Zero*</u>, okay.

*(More mumbling.)*

*(Into the headset.)* You *do* want the Onion Thrills, okay sure.

*(More mumbling. Then:)*

*(Into the headset; eye-roll.)* Your total's gonna be $25.82, please pull up to the second window.

*(She's about to put the headset down when:)*

*(More mumbling.)*

*(Into the headset.)* Well. Maybe not ninety nifty seconds *guaranteed*, but –

*(More mumbling.)*

*(Into the headset.)* Right, I'm aware that's our thing. But I'm the only one working tonight, so –

*(More mumbling.)*

*(Into the headset.)* Because it's Christmas Eve.

*(More mumbling.)*

*(Into the headset.)* That's what the sign on the door says, yes.

*(More mumbling.)*

*(Into the headset.)* And that's the phone number to the feedback hotline, yes.

*(Beat. A moment.)*

*(More mumbling as* **MARGOT** *looks towards the kitchen. Can she do this? She can do this.)*

*(Into the headset.)* You know what?

That won't be necessary.

*(Beat.)*

*(À la "challenge accepted.")* You want ninety nifty seconds? I'll give you ninety *nifty* seconds. Guaranteed.

*(***MARGOT*** quickly throws off the headset as she jumps over the counter into the kitchen space. Speed. Racer. Mode.)*

*(She tosses frozen Onion Thrills into the fryer, pulls out patties like they were on fire, condiments go flying…)*

*(The car pulls up to the drive-thru window.* **MARGOT** *pauses, hops over the kitchen counter to the register, opens the drive-thru window.)*

$25.82.

*(She reaches for a debit card, takes it, swipes that VISA like she's Swiper the Swiper, pulls the receipt out as it prints, and tosses it carelessly into the car.)*

There you go!

*(She hops back over the kitchen counter. Beeping from the fryer, she lifts the gate and dumps the Onion Thrills into the metal salt thing.)*

*(She tops each sandwich/burger with their appropriate bun, wraps them in their matching wrapper, and tosses them into an already opened to-go bag like she were Kobe [Rest in Power].)*

*(She scoops Texas Twirls and Onion Thrills, tosses those as well, closes the bag, grabs the drinks, hops over the counter once more, and makes it just in the nick of time.)*

*(Sweaty; breathless.)* Here you go, sir. Ninety *nifty* seconds. Guaranteed. Just an FYI you'll probably wanna pop those Onion Thrills in the microwave for like three minutes 'cause they might still be a little frozen. Okay, thank you so much, have a Very Merry Happy Burger Christmas, goodbye!

*(And just like that, **MARGOT** closes the window to the drive thru and the car drives off.)*

*(Sweet, pure relief.)* Woo! Take *that* Dodge charger.

*(The tree and fallen ornaments twinkle.)*

Oh right. Almost forgot about you.

*(**MARGOT** heads to the back room, grabs a broom, and sweeps.)*

It never ends.

*(Maybe a minute of this, watching her sweep...)*

*(Grabbing the dustpan...)*

*(Sweeping the mess into the dustpan when something outside catches her eye.)*

Not *this* guy again.

*(Shouting towards the door:)* Hey! HEY!

> *(***MARGOT*** *unlocks and opens the door to the outside world.)*

> *(Yelling outside.)*

This is private property, you can't just leave your stuff here – I don't care how cold it is! If you don't get up and out, I'll have to call the cops! That's right, you BETTER walk away! MERRY CHRISTMAS!

> *(She slams the door shut, locks it.)*

*(To herself.)* God these homeless are like friggin cockroaches!

> *(***MARGOT*** *grabs the dustpan from earlier, empties the broken ornament pieces in the trashcan.)*

> *(There's a ***ROBOTIC GRUMPY SANTA CLAUS*** toy close by. It turns on, unprompted. Scares the shit out of* ***MARGOT****:)*

**ROBOTIC SANTA.**  "Back off! / It's been a *rough* year for Santa!"

**MARGOT.**  *Waaah!* You scared me!

> *(She walks towards it – hesitant. She squeezes his hand, trying to get him to talk again. Nothing.)*

*(Frustrated.)* Aw come on –

> *(She grabs ***SANTA****. Shakes him.)*

> *(Then:)*

**ROBOTIC SANTA.**  "I'm always watching you!"

**MARGOT.** *(To* **SANTA.***)* God, you're so old. Rode hard and put away wet.

> *(She sets him back down on the counter.)*

**ROBOTIC SANTA.** "Bah Humbug!"

**MARGOT.** *(Chuckles.)* Right back atcha Grumpy.

> *(***MARGOT***'s phone vibrates. She checks the text on her phone. Heavy sigh.)*

*(To* **SANTA.***)* You got a cousin? No? Just you and Mrs. Claus and a couple of ugly elves?

> *(Her phone vibrates again. Another text. She motions her cell phone.)*

*(To* **SANTA.***)* I got a cousin. Letty. Every year she throws this _huge_ Christmas Eve party full of people I don't even know.

> *(Then:)*

She has a lot of friends. Me? Not so much.

*(Texting back via voice dictation.)* "Sorry, can't make it (period). Working (period). Merry Xmas (period). Sad face."

> *(She sends her text.)*

> *(Beat. A moment.)*

> *(Another vibration, indicating a response.)*

> *(***MARGOT*** *reads it.)*

*(To* **SANTA.***)* Damn she got conchas from El Bolillo.

> *(Then, another vibration.* **MARGOT** *reads it.)*

*(Reading.)* "I never see you anymore."

*(To* **SANTA.***)* Seriously? It's not like I don't *wanna* be there, I'm just working.

*(Beat. Side eye from* **SANTA.***)*

*(Texting back via voice dictation.)* "Yeah (comma), sorry (period) Got lots on my plate right now (dot dot dot)…"

*(She hits send. Anxiously waits for a response.)*

*(Phone notification.)*

*(Her face says it all.)*

*(Reading.)* "Your mom would want you to be here."

*(Beat.)*

*(Texting back via voice dictation.)* "Funny coming from someone who barely saw her (exclamation mark)!"

*(She hits send. Then:)*

*(To* **SANTA.***)* Oh she's typing.

*(Waits anxiously.)*

*(To* **SANTA.***)* Still typing…

*(Waits some more. Then:)*

*(To* **SANTA.***)* She stopped.

No response.

Wow. Okay.

*(She puts away her phone.)*

*(To* **SANTA.***)* It's one dinner. With people who *literally* only see each other once a year. And their ugly kids. And their sad sweaters.

*(The "ding" sound of a car pulling up to the drive-thru window is heard and then –)*

**RAÚL**.  *(Voice-over. <u>Too</u> cheerful.)* Howdy! Hola! Bonjour! Welcome to Happy Burger! This is Raúl speaking, founder and President of Joy, bringing you Crispy Cheer with every bite since –

> *(**MARGOT** gets to the headset and hits the intercom button before the recording finishes. Annoyed:)*

**MARGOT**.  *(Into the headset; not Happy.)* Welcome to Happy Burger, proud home of the Happy Burger, where the burgers are hot and the holiday spirit is Happy-sized, would you like to try our Merry & Bright Happy Burger Combo today?

> *(Beat. A moment. Nothing.)*

Is the intercom broken?

> *(She tries again.)*

*(Into the headset; more UnHappy.)* Welcome to Happy Burger, can I take your order?

> *(A moment. Nothing.)*

> *(She tries again.)*

*(Into the headset.)* Hello?

Hello, hello?

> *(She leans over the drive-thru window to see if there's anyone there. There isn't.)*

Mother trucker must've drove off.

> *(She takes off her headset and heads back to the cardboard boxes. Begins unpacking.)*

*(Then, the "ding" sound of the drive thru is heard again.)*

*(To herself.)* What the heck?!

**RAÚL.** *(Voice-over. <u>Too</u> cheerful.)* Howdy! Hola! Bonjour! Welcome to –

*(**MARGOT** hits the intercom –)*

**MARGOT.** *(Into the headset; not Happy.)* Welcome to Happy Burger, proud home of the Happy Burger –

*(The sound of the drive-thru "ding" cuts her off.)*

Okay this isn't funny –

*(Ding, ding, ding, ding –)*

*(She opens the drive-thru window, leans over it again – there's no one there.)*

Huh?

*(Ding, ding, ding, ding – it's incessant and won't stop as if cars are driving through it in rapid succession.)*

*(Into the headset.)* Hello hello hello –

*(Ding, ding, ding, ding –)*

*(Then –)*

*(The power goes out, pitch black.)*

Oh hell no.

*(Schum! The red bulbs of the Christmas light decorations turn on, an ominous red glow like a Christmas hellscape.)*

(*Then, a* **BOOMING CHOLA VOICE** *bursts from the headset into the ether, bouncing against the walls:*)

JACKIE/BOOMING VOICE.  MARGOT!!!!!

(**MARGOT** *screams.*)

MARGOT.  Who's there?!

(**MARGOT** *jumps behind the counter, hiding. But from what?*)

JACKIE/BOOMING VOICE.  MARGOT!!!!

(**MARGOT** *is in shock.*)

MARGOT.  What is going on?!

JACKIE/BOOMING VOICE.  MARGARITA ADELINA MAYDENITA CHIHUAHUITA ADELANTE SABADO GIGANTE MUÑOZ! ALSO KNOWN AS *MARRRGGGOOOOTTTT*!

MARGOT.  Who are you?! What do you want?!

JACKIE/BOOMING VOICE.  YOU DON'T RECOGNIZE ME?!

(*Beat.*)

MARGOT.  (*Obvious:*) No!

(*Then,* **MARGOT** *is thrust to her feet as the spirit of* **JACKIE/THE BOOMING VOICE** *is thrust into her through her belly button, making her way through* **MARGOT**'s *body, veins, pores.*)

(*She is possessed.*)

(*She takes a moment, looks around.*)

(*As* **JACKIE***: late teens, hood as fuck, big hoops, witty with a potty mouth and doesn't give a fuck what you think.*)

**JACKIE.** (*As if she saw her at a party.*) Hey bitch! Did you miss me?

(*Beat. A moment. She belches. A shift back into* **MARGOT**.)

**MARGOT.** Jackie?! Oh my god! What the – but how can you –

(*Another shift.*)

**JACKIE.** Remember that time after work (?) I took you to see *The Exorcist* with me at Hermann Park?

**MARGOT.** How could I forget? I had nightmares for like a week.

**JACKIE.** So this is a lot like that *PERO*...without the vomit.

(*Beat. A moment.*)

**MARGOT.** So I'm possessed?

**JACKIE.** Yah huh.

**MARGOT.** Right now?

**JACKIE.** Yeah.

**MARGOT.** But... How?

**JACKIE.** Bitch! You ask too many questions. Besides, where's the fun without a little mystery?

**MARGOT.** You know I don't like mysteries.

**JACKIE.** But you *love* surprises...

**MARGOT.** Not like this! This feels...different. Weird. Like. I have all this...energy all of a sudden.

**JACKIE.** Well yeah bitch. I'm seventeen and you old as fuck.

**MARGOT.** (*Worries she's old.*) I'm not old!

**JACKIE**. You old to me.

**MARGOT**. I can't believe I'm talking to you right now. Well, kind of. You know what I –

**JACKIE**. Yeah.

**MARGOT**. Because you're –

**JACKIE**. Yeah, no yeah.

**MARGOT**. And I'm –

**JACKIE**. Yeah, for sure, yeah –

**MARGOT**. <u>Yeah</u>! But, like...*why* are you here?

**JACKIE**. What is this, the Spanish Inquisition? Can't a bitch visit her Happy Burger work wifey without the third degree, fuck!

**MARGOT**. No of course, you can, I'm really glad you're here, actually. It's just...don't spirits come with, like, an intention or something? A message, or whatever?

**JACKIE**. Bitch! You watch way too much *Hollywood Medium*. You need to chillax. Here.

(**JACKIE** *pulls out a blunt from her pocket.*)

**MARGOT**. Jackie! You know we're not supposed to be doing that! Where did you get this?

**JACKIE**. *(While licking the joint.)* Shhhh, just a little. To take the edge off.

**MARGOT**. No no no no I don't do that anymore, not since you –

(**JACKIE** *lights the joint, inhales a puff.*)

Died.

(*It's too late. Relaxed now. A moment. Then:*)

You're right. I do feel better.

*(They laugh hysterically. The kind of laugh you laugh when you are high kind of laugh.)*

Can I ask you something?

**JACKIE.** Duh bitch.

**MARGOT.** Did it...hurt? When it happened.

*(Beat. A moment. Then:)*

**JACKIE.** You know, it didn't hurt as bad as I looked. The whole thing was just tragic.

**MARGOT.** You saw the campaign that came out of it right?

**JACKIE.** I *did* see it. That was real nice. "Look Left. Look Right. Look Alive." Clever.

**MARGOT.** It's still a mess, though.

**JACKIE.** Whoever thought putting a light rail at street level is stupid as <u>fuck</u>. Period.

**MARGOT.** I'm surprised they let you drop F-bombs in heaven. Or, you know, wherever you are.

**JACKIE.** Why wouldn't they?

**MARGOT.** Well, there's gotta be a lot of pretty important people up there.

**JACKIE.** *(Annoyed.)* Uh huh.

**MARGOT.** So I just thought there might be like, rules or decorum or something.

**JACKIE.** On how to talk?

**MARGOT.** Exactly.

**JACKIE.** But why would you think that?

**MARGOT.** Because <u>some</u> people may find your use of profanity as lazy, and boring, and only vaguely amusing. I don't. But some people might.

*(Beat.)*

*(**JACKIE** takes another hit.)*

**JACKIE**.  Shakespeare cussed.

**MARGOT**.  Since when do you read Shakespeare?

**JACKIE**.  I don't. But we kick it every now and then. You know. In "heaven."

**MARGOT**.  I have a really hard time believing that.

**JACKIE**.  He doesn't use the same words as me, but he definitely talks shit. You see, Margot. Some people – people like *you* – limit your ways of thinking. Because when you think about it, like really, really, *really* think about it? The way I talk *is* Shakespearean, bitch. It's heightened. It has a flow to it, a rhythm to it, a musicality to it, the way it rolls off the tongue. So when I call you a "bitch ass hoe," that means I really think you a <u>muthafuckin bitch ass hoe</u>. I say what I mean, and I mean what I say. You know what I mean? Very Shakespeare.

*(Beat. A moment. Then:)*

Fuck dude, you got my blood pressure all up and shit.

*(She takes another hit.)*

**MARGOT**.  I'm sorry, Jackie. I didn't mean to upset you.

**JACKIE**.  Yeah well you did. Which is weird given all the shit we been through. I mean, <u>I'm</u> the one who trained ya ass for fuck's sake. We really had somethin', Margot. We were tight. We did everything together. *(Nodding.)* Working together by the fryers, trying not to burn my hair extensions... Helping me at the register when I'd get a new set of acrylics... Shit, I even taught you how to clean the grease trap without crying, and *that's* something only the *family* knows, which means I really fucking loved you, bitch.

*(Beat. A moment. Then:)*

**MARGOT.** You ever think about how things might've been different for us? You know, if you were still here?

**JACKIE.** All the time. We'd practically be running this place.

**MARGOT.** Yeah. Maybe.

**JACKIE.** Raúl wouldn't know what to do with us.

**MARGOT.** Yeah, it's not like he knew what to do with me from the start, so.

*(Beat. A moment. Something deeper there.)*

**JACKIE.** Margot. I know the year we worked together was tough. With your mom in and out of the hospital and shit?

**MARGOT.** Are we really talking about my mom right now?

**JACKIE.** You're the one who brought it up.

**MARGOT.** No. I didn't.

**JACKIE.** Then maybe we should.

Cancer's an ugly disease, Margot.

**MARGOT.** I know, I had a front row seat to it.

**JACKIE.** Then you should also know that when she died of it, and when you pushed everyone away *because* of it, that that's part of the ugliness too. It was like working with a total stranger all of a sudden, even after a whole year of us being work wifeys. And then *I* died, and well – talk about buzz kill, am I right?

**MARGOT.** What are you saying?

**JACKIE.** I'm *saying* that I thought you would've moved on by now, that's all.

**MARGOT.** Says the girl who's back from the dead.

JACKIE. I might be the one who's dead, but at least I knew how to *live*. Don't you wanna live, bitch? Drive a Ferrari, drink some Bacardi, act like you Cardi? Don't you think it's time to, like...I dunno. Let someone *else* work the night shift before Christmas, you dumb bitch? I mean, no one likes working this shift but you, Margot. And truth be told, even *before* I died, I always thought that was a little sad. Even Crackhead Carlos called in sick tonight, and that's saying a lot.

(*Beat. A moment. Then:*)

You know I love you, right?

MARGOT. (*A little sad.*) Yeah...

JACKIE. Okay good. 'Cause this is the part of the story where I tell you why I'm *actually* here and I don't want you to be mad at me for it. Okay?

MARGOT. Okay...

JACKIE. Somebody on the other side said, "visit Margot, she needs a wake up call" so here I am, and here it is: Tonight, you're going to be visited by four spirits, and the first is me bitch. (Obviously.) And I just came by to tell you that I'm just the first but won't be the last and it's about to be Freaky Friday up in this bitch.

(*Beat.*)

Okay byeeeeeeeeee.

MARGOT. Wait don't go!

(*Beat. A moment.*)

Who sent you here? Who else is coming?

JACKIE. I can't tell you that!

MARGOT. So I'm just supposed to sit around and wait for whoever, *when*ever they decide to show up?! I can't do that! I have a *job*. You know I can't be worrying about this.

**JACKIE.** Well you're gonna have to. And the longer it takes for you to accept that, the bumpier the ride this night shift is gonna be.

> (*Beat. A moment. As if she were about to leave –*)

Oh, one last thing. She wanted me to tell you that she's coming for you.

So you better be ready for it, like *Game of Thrones* because Winter is coming for you, Margot. She's coming. She is.

> (*Beat.*)

Bitch.

> (*Then,* **MARGOT** *belches and* **JACKIE** *is released back into the wind. The restaurant goes back to normal.*)

> (**MARGOT** *desperately gasps for air.*)

**MARGOT.** Oh my god I think I'm gonna be sick.

> (*Beat. A moment. Then, like she were chasing her spirit –*)

Jackie? Jackie come back. Who's coming for me? Who's coming?!

> (**SANTA** *comes to life.*)

**ROBOTIC SANTA.** *"Get your own free stuff!"*

**MARGOT.** (*Startled.*) Ah!

> (**SANTA** *starts laughing in the robotic way it does, begging for her attention.*)

Yeah, screw this!

(*She throws herself over the counter, grabs her tote bag.* **SANTA** *keeps laughing maniacally. The "ding" from the drive-thru window can be heard.*)

(*Then, the voice recording of Raúl. But this time the voice sounds distorted, demonic, horrifying:*)

**RAÚL.**  (*Voice-over.*) *Welcome to Happy Burger, bringing you Crispy Cheer with every bite since 1979!!!*

**MARGOT.**  Get me outta here!

(*She throws herself back over the counter and is almost at the exit when an invisible force pulls her back into the restaurant, her tote bag thrown across the room.*)

Not again!

(*Then,* **MARGOT** *starts convulsing. Seizure-like. It's horrific, like in a movie, until it slowly turns into a hula-hoop interpretative dance. Then it's hysterical. Completely unreal.*)

(*She's possessed.*)

(*A moment.*)

(*Then –*)

(*As* **CLYDE**: *mid-fifties. Member of the Choir at Immaculate Heart of Mary. An introverted extrovert who loves performing but hates audiences. He's got a Texas drawl to him.*)

**CLYDE.**  (*Singing; country-style.*)
AWAY IN A MANGER, NO CRIB FOR A BED.

(*He coughs, clears his throat.*)

Sorry wrong key. I started too low.

*(He clears his throat, starts again.)*

AWAY IN A MANGER, NO CRIB FOR A BED.
THE LITTLE LORD JESUS LAID DOWN HIS SWEET HEAD.
THE STARS IN THE SKY LOOK DOWN WHERE HE LAY.
THE LITTLE LORD JESUS ASLEEP ON THE HAY.

*(Beat. A moment.)*

Howdy Miss Margot.

**MARGOT**.  Who the heck are you?!

**CLYDE**.  Woah there Nelly, you talk to your mother with that attitude?

**MARGOT**.  She's dead so no. I don't.

**CLYDE**.  *(Realizes he made a mistake.)* Oh no. Oh my big ol' mouth, I'm so sorry about that Miss.

**MARGOT**.  No Miss. Just Margot.

**CLYDE**.  Margot. That's a funny name. I like it.

*(He wipes his hand clean, extends it for a handshake.)*

Name's Clyde. Howdy.

**MARGOT**.  Hi.

*(**CLYDE** makes himself comfortable.)*

**CLYDE**.  Oooh, it's cozy in here. Nice, and warm… little cold right by your chest, though. Splash a warm whiskey always melts a cold heart…

**MARGOT**.  I don't drink.

**CLYDE**.  I'm sorry. For a second there, I thought you said you <u>don't</u> drink.

**MARGOT**.  That is correct.

**CLYDE.** *(Thinks he's intuiting something.)* Ohhhhhh. I see.

*(Whispers.)* You're one of them alcoholics.

*(Tender.)* It's okay. You're in good company.

*(He winks.)*

**MARGOT.**  I'm not an alcoholic. I just don't like the taste. Especially whiskey, it's disgusting.

**CLYDE.**  Disgusting?! Well what kinda whiskey are you drinking there, Miss Margot? Cow piss?!

*(**CLYDE** pulls out a flask.)*

Here. Try this.

**MARGOT.**  No, no, no, no, no –

*(Too late. He's already poured a healthy gulp down **MARGOT**'s throat. She shakes it off.)*

Woo! That was...that was...

**CLYDE.**  That was William Larue Weller, thank you very much.

**MARGOT.**  He tastes pretty good.

**CLYDE.**  I got the good stuff! Just holler if you ever want a little. Goes great with your coffee. Oh! You know who has good coffee? Immaculate Heart of Mary. 'Specially at their AA meetings on Sundays. You ever been to Immaculate Heart of Mary? The one right across the way over there?

**MARGOT.**  Can't say I have.

**CLYDE.**  I sing in the choir. Well, sometimes. Mostly around Christmas. And Easter. I'm what the people there call a "Cafeteria Catholic."

**MARGOT.**  What's a Cafeteria Catholic?

**CLYDE.**  A Cafeteria Catholic is someone who picks and chooses what parts to keep, and what parts to skip. You know. Like in a Cafeteria.

**MARGOT.**  Interesting. And you're okay with people calling you that?

**CLYDE.**  I don't mind. I'm too much of a sinner to be considered anything else, I reckon.

*(Humble.)* I'm a gambler.

**MARGOT.**  Of course you are.

**CLYDE.**  You always judge a book by its cover, Margot?

**MARGOT.**  No.

**CLYDE.**  Sure didn't sound that way to me. And it sure as heck didn't sound that way when you were talkin' to that "homeless cockroach" from off the street.

*(Beat.)*

Yeah I heard ya. And that wasn't the first time you been talkin' to him that way either. Like he ain't got better things to do than be berated by people like you. He needs *help*.

**MARGOT.**  No he doesn't. He's homeless because he wants to be homeless.

**CLYDE.**  I saw you last week, you know. When you went out there and told that man off, somethin' nasty.

**MARGOT.**  *(Slightly embarrassed.)* I didn't tell him off.

**CLYDE.**  I may be a gambler and I may (or may not) be an Anonymous Alcoholic but if there's one thing I'm *not*, it's blind <u>or</u> a liar. And right now you tryin' to make it sound like I'm both. I know what I saw. I was sittin' on this here table over here eatin' my Happy Burger with extra Secret Happy Sauce when you went over to that man who was doin' nuthin' but mindin' his own business on the street, not doin' nothin' to nobody, and you just go over to him and start yellin' at him, <u>tellin' him off</u>, sayin' he's gotta get outta here or you'll call the cops.

*(Beat. A moment.)*

**CLYDE**. You like calling the cops on people just minding their own business?

**MARGOT**. No.

**CLYDE**. Sheesh. Sometimes, these cops be so stupid, they just start shootin' without even lookin' at who they might be shootin' at.

> *(Then:)*

So I went over to talk to him. Followed him after <u>you</u> told him to leave. And I tapped him on the shoulder and he turned around and we just stood there. Noticing each other. And I could feel his soul reverberating against mine like we was destined to be there, on the corner of the street outside this Happy Burger, when god as my witness…it started to snow. In the middle of the day, Snow. In Texas! Like a miracle, or something. Wasn't enough to stick around but man…it was somethin'. So I looked at him – my Happy Burger falling out of my hands – Secret Special Happy Sauce drippin' wet and warm between the cracks of my fingers, and I said, "You wanna split it?" I would have bought him his own but I was broke as shit from Titty Tuesday, with nuthin' more than ten dollars to my name. And to put it honestly, I shoulda saved those ten bucks to cover electricity or somethin' but –

> *(Beat; a pivot.)*

You know that kinda hungry you get that feels like a big black hole in the pit of your stomach? The type of hunger that is so darn loud you got no choice but to stop everything you're doing so you can tend to that hunger? *That's* how hungry I was. And by the looks on this young man's face, I could tell he was blacked out hangry, too. So I cut my Happy Burger in half with my hands and offered him the bigger piece. "Here. Take it. Eat this in memory of me."

*(**CLYDE** pulls out a burger from his pocket. He cuts it in half.)*

*(Beat. A shift. **MARGOT** is now the "homeless man.")*

*(She/he looks at the burger half hesitantly… then – she/he devours it like she/he hadn't eaten in days. Which could very well be the case.)*

**MARGOT**.  *(As if she were the homeless man.)* Thank you.

I'm Rico.

**CLYDE**.  Howdy, Rico. Name's Clyde.

**RICO**.  Hi Clyde.

**CLYDE**.  How old are you Rico?

**RICO**.  I'm twenty-five. No, twenty-six. Yeah, I'm twenty-six.

**CLYDE**.  You're a little young to be wanderin' around here by your lonesome.

**RICO**.  I got nothin', man. Nothin'. I keep tryin' to find my family but I don't know how to get to Downtown L.A. I think I might be lost?

(Then:)

Can you tell me how to get to Downtown L.A.? My family's expecting me. Have you heard from them at all?

*(Beat. A moment. He takes another bite. Then:)*

Where am I?

**CLYDE**.  You're in Texas. Houston, Texas.

**RICO**.  Oh. Okay. How far is that from L.A.?

**CLYDE**.  Pretty far.

(**RICO** *nods his head, taking this in.*)

**RICO.** Okay. Yeah. Texas. Right, okay.

(*He takes another bite, pushing through his confusion, the mental illness that got him here in the first place. Then:*)

This is really good, man. Thank you.

**CLYDE.** (*To* **MARGOT.**) And as he's eating this Happy Burger, the snow is falling down, *hard,* and I put my hands in my pockets because they're startin' to get cold, and I feel a texture that feels familiar to me. So I pull it out and it's a hundred dollar bill. I was so darn blasted from Titty Tuesday, I completely forgot I saved it secret in my pocket 'cause I knew that future me, sober me, would be needin' it to keep the lights on in that damn ol' trailer of mine. And so I'm staring at this money, broke as shit. Staring at this man, staring at me, staring at this moment, also broke as shit. And it's so tense, so quiet, I could hear each snowflake shatterin' on my shoulder as it touched me. And like the Holy Ghost possessed me or somethin', I reached out to him and said, "Here. You take it."

**RICO.** (*Shocked.*) Are you serious?

**CLYDE.** Yeah. Take it. Merry Christmas.

(**RICO** *takes the money.*)

**RICO.** Thanks man.

(*Beat. A moment. Then:*)

God, you look so familiar to me.

(*Then; a realization.*)

Wait. You were you singin' at that church! The one across the street!

**CLYDE.** *(Laughing.)* Immaculate Heart, yeup. I'm a choir boy. Well, sometimes.

**RICO.** They were giving out food last Sunday so I stopped by and some guys that looked and sounded kinda funny like you were all singin' and dancin' together, it was nice. I remember you the most. You looked the funniest to me. When you sang, I mean.

**CLYDE.** What song was your favorite?

**RICO.** Oh, that's easy. The last one with the big finale. Where the whole choir came together and did a bunch of little dance moves? I like that one a lot.

(**CLYDE** *smiles, touched.*)

**CLYDE.** That's my favorite one, too.

**RICO.** I don't know how you do it, making it look like magic.

**CLYDE.** Aw, it's not that hard. All's you need is a good two-step.

**RICO.** *(Chuckling.)* Yeah, I can't do one of those.

**CLYDE.** Sure you can! I can teach ya.

**RICO.** You wanna teach me how to two step? Right now?

**CLYDE.** No better time than the present. How about it, Rico? May I have this dance?

*(To* **MARGOT**.*)* So I extend my hand towards his. And he takes it, ever so gently within mine as if he could break any minute, or somethin', like a snowflake. And then…like the holy spirit never left…I teach him the dance.

(**MARGOT** *[as* **CLYDE***] claps her hands and the lights shift and glow, as a country version of a popular Christmas song [something like*

*Kacey Musgraves' cover of "Feliz Navidad"]
plays over the restaurant overhead speaker.*)*

*(She pulls out a cowboy hat from somewhere
and grabs her belt loop as she takes the
position.)*

*(Then –)*

*(She does an elaborate Texas-style line dance
to the tune.)*

*(It's stunning.)*

*(Impeccable.)*

*(Looks like she could have been a professional
dancer in her past life, how good this looks.
Then –)*

*(Big. Climactic. Finish.)*

*(Thunderous applause, she bows. Lights shift
back. As she catches her breath:)*

**CLYDE.**  And when I finished teachin' him the dance, *ooo-
wey!* I've never seen a smile that big before. We were
laughin' and dancin' and singin'. Swear to god, I think
I might've farted once or twice!

---

* A license to produce *The Night Shift Before Christmas* does not include
a performance license for "Feliz Navidad" by Kacey Musgraves. The
publisher and author suggest that the licensee contact ASCAP or BMI
to ascertain the music publisher and contact such music publisher to
license or acquire permission for performance of the song. If a license
or permission is unattainable, the licensee may not use the song in *The
Night Shift Before Christmas* but should create an original composition
in a similar style or use a similar song in the public domain. For further
information, please see the Music and Third-Party Materials Use Note
on page iii.

*(He laughs.)*

But I didn't fart. I died. Yup. Right there, on the sidewalk, just outside this Happy Burger. Abdominal aortic aneurysm, I'll come to find out. Just...*pop!* Like a fart. You never know when your last meal will be your last so you better enjoy every darn bite.

*(Beat.)*

**MARGOT**. *(A realization.)* Oh my god. You're the guy. That that that *dead* guy, the guy who died like – that was like –

**CLYDE**.  Three days ago. Mhmm. And now, he is risen.

**MARGOT**.  I'm the one who found you. After work? I remember passing you on the sidewalk thinking... damn that's sad. Just laying out there in the melted snow like that?

**CLYDE**.  Didn't feel a thing when it happened. Nothing more than that butterfly, bubbly, warm but also sad feelin' in my lower back. I felt like I saw Jesus right before I went out, though. Or maybe it was just Rico's face of horror as I passed out, it's hard to say.

*(Then; to clarify.)*

He looked a lot like the big J man, if you ask me.

**MARGOT**.  I didn't even wait for the ambulance after I called 911. I just...left you there and went home.

*(Beat. **MARGOT** thinks on this.)*

You're a good person. Me? I'm not that good.

**CLYDE**.  You really think that poorly about yourself?

**MARGOT**.  I mean, I left you in a pile of melted snow. Alone.

*(Beat.)*

**CLYDE.** Yeah you're definitely not that good a person, Margot. But you also don't have to stay that way. The world needs more good people in it. Because without good people, well... I don't know what will happen to guys like Rico. A small act of loving kindness goes a long way, Miss Margot. So next time you find a dead guy on the street, maybe wait with him till the ambulance arrives. You know. So he isn't alone. And so his drawers don't get soaked and soiled from melted snow and dog piss.

**MARGOT.** I'll keep that in mind. I can't make any promises though.

Especially if I'm running late to work.

**CLYDE.** *(Nodding.)* That's fair.

*(Beat. A twinkle of some kind.)*

I think it's time I get outta dodge.

**MARGOT.** What? Already?

**CLYDE.** 'fraid so.

*(He gathers his things, preparing to go.* **MARGOT** *doesn't know what to do with the sudden emptiness she's feeling.)*

Oh, but one last thing? She uh...wanted me to tell you somethin', Margot.

**MARGOT.** Okay...

*(Beat. A moment.)*

**CLYDE.** SHE'S A COMIN'! ...

*(Then, a loud belch escapes* **MARGOT***'s lips. And just like that,* **CLYDE** *is gone.)*

**MARGOT.** *(Shouting at the spirit.)* WHO THE HECK IS COMING?!

*(She takes a step, almost collapses. Her legs feel like Jell-O.)*

*(Re: her legs.)* Ow ow ow ow ow ow ow ow ow – I didn't even know my legs could *do* all that! Oh, did I get my steps in?!

*(She checks her Fitbit.)*

*(Disappointed.)* No.

*(To* **SANTA***; reflective.)* Small acts of loving kindness...

*(Beat. A moment. Then:)*

Well that's the stupidest thing I've ever heard. I don't see anyone lookin' out for *me*. Why should I do the same? In this economy?

*(She walks back towards the broom but stops herself as her eye catches something. She walks over to the front doors of the restaurant.)*

*(Childlike awe.)* Ohmygoodness, look, Grumpy Santa. It's snowing. It probably won't stick but it sure is pretty huh.

*(Then:)*

Geez, it's gettin' colder out.

*(Beat.)*

You think that guy's okay?

*(Beat. No response.)*

Santa?

*(Still nothing. She walks back over to the* **SANTA***. Then – he dances, unprompted.)*

**ROBOTIC SANTA.** *"Are you on the nice list, little girl? Or have you been naughty?"*

*(Beat.)*

**MARGOT**.  *(To* **SANTA**.*)* There's something you're not telling me, Mr. Grumpy.

> *(He stares at her.)*

> *(The sound of the "ding" in the drive-thru window.)*

Oh Lord. Here we go again.

> *(She covers her eyes with her hands, in fear. It's like that moment of anticipation before getting a vaccine or the first time they pull a wax strip from your hoo-hah. But then –)*

**RAÚL**.  *(Voice-over.* <u>*Too*</u> *cheerful.)* Howdy! Hola! Bonjour! Welcome to Happy Burger! This is Raúl speaking, founder and President of Joy, bringing you Crispy Cheer with every bite since 1979. Hang tight – someone will be with you shortly. Ciao!

> *(A moment. Then – we hear a noise come from her headset:)*

**CUSTOMER**.  *(Heard from Margot's headset; mumbling.)* Hello? Anybody there?

**MARGOT**.  Oh snap. A real customer!

> *(She rushes over to the headset –)*

*(In the headset.)* Hi there, sorry. Welcome to Happy Burger, proud home of the Happy Burger, where the burgers are excited and the holiday spirit is Happy-sized. Would you like to try our Merry & Bright Happy Burger Combo today, only available for a limited time?

> *(Mumbling from the headset. Then:)*

*(In the headset.)* Uh huh.

*(Beat. A moment. Mumbling.)*

*(In the headset.)* I'm sorry, our soft serve machine is down.

> *(Loud mumbling. She takes a sip from her drink.)*

*(In the headset.)* No milkshakes either, I'm afraid.

> *(Loud mumbling. Yelling.)*

*(In the headset.)* Okay, fine. Go to Whataburger, I don't care, tell them I say "hi"!

> *(The car speeds away. She throws off her headset.)*

Jackass. Some people, man...

> *(**SANTA** comes to life.)*

**ROBOTIC SANTA.** *"She's coming..."*

**MARGOT.** *(To **SANTA**.)* What?

**ROBOTIC SANTA.** *"Bah Humbug!"*

> *(Another "ding" can be heard from the drive thru. She knows what this means.)*

**MARGOT.** Jesus take the wheel.

> *(Without missing a beat, **MARGOT** starts convulsing again. The same seizure-like, hula-hoop-type dance movement sequence.)*

> *(As this happens, the overhead lights blow out leaving just the Christmas lights on, glowing hauntingly, setting the scene for what's about to come. **MARGOT** is possessed...or is she? She looks normal, sounds normal...)*

*(Then, suddenly, her hands pull her across the restaurant over to the counter as if they had a life of their own to where a piano keyboard appears like magic.)*

*(She snaps her fingers – sole spotlight as if she were the star of her own intimate concert. Because she is. She pulls a bedazzled mic out of a styrofoam cup and attaches it to something nearby as she gets on the piano, plucking keys.)*

*(She musically improvises on the piano as the spirit inside her comes to life and addresses us like we were her captivated audience somewhere magical like the House of Blues or the backyard of your tía's carne asada.)*

*(As **GRACIE**: late twenties. A fierce performer, a vulnerable heart, a free spirit. Someone who cares deeply about what other people think, but also someone who pretends not to.)*

**GRACIE.**  Is everybody having a good time tonight?

*(She pauses for cheers.)*

I said...*is everyone having a good time tonight?!*

*(The audience cheers louder. She smiles, laughs.)*

There you go. If I didn't know any better, I swear all y'all were dead! Or maybe it's just me.

*(She laughs at her own joke.)*

Anyway. Wow. Tonight has been so special. You know, late at night when all the world is sleeping, I stay up and think about a night like this. It's what I've always dreamed of.

*(She closes her eyes, still plucking keys, taking it all in. A moment. Then:)*

For this last one, I wrote a little something for the holidays. Now y'all know me, I'm not one to write Christmas songs but I was inspired by a man I met on the night train to Venice. His name was Carlo Bertogno and yes, he was as sexy as his name sounds. One look in his eyes and it was over. I was smitten. And so was he.

*(Beat as she remembers. Then:)*

Carlo, wherever you are in the world, baby, this one's for you.

*(More piano. Some sass to it.)*

*And* for the dolls. The girlies. Girls like me, girls like <u>us</u>, who have loved and lost and would do it all over again, if we could. This is "Christmas, Just Like."

*(Playing; singing.)*

I'M SUPPOSED TO WRITE ABOUT CHRISTMAS.
BUT INSTEAD, I THINK I'LL WRITE ABOUT YOU.
WATCH THE ROAD, IT FEELS JUST LIKE CHRISTMAS
WHENEVER WE'RE TOGETHER, IT'S TRUE.

THE WARMTH BY YOUR FIRE,
YOUR ARMS LIKE A BLANKET,
A CHILDLIKE DESIRE,
A SANTA SO SECRET

NOW THESE BLUES
CINDY-UH-LOU –
BECAUSE I WON'T BE SPENDING
CHRISTMAS WITH YOU.

ONE DAY GOES BY SINCE I LAST SAW YOUR FACE
TWO DAYS, AND THEN THREE, AND THEN TEN
AND I CAN'T SEEM TO GET YOU OUT OF MY HEAD
YOU'VE TRAPPED ME IN YOUR HOUSE OF GINGERBREAD.

WHERE YOU SPUN ME AROUND
IN THE COLD, CRISPY NIGHT
ON THAT DECK BACK IN DENVER
GOT THAT LOOK IN YOUR EYES
JUST LIKE CHRISTMAS.

I SWEAR, THAT NIGHT FELT LIKE CHRISTMAS
IN YOUR ARMS, JUST LIKE CHRISTMAS
MY HANDS IN YOUR HAIR, JUST LIKE CHRISTMAS
THE WAY YOU WOULD STARE, CALL ME CHRISTMAS
I WAS THERE, YOU WERE THERE, WE WERE THERE

*(Instrumentation. We think the song is over.
But then:)*

ONE DAY GOES BY SINCE I LAST SAW YOUR FACE.
TWO DAYS, AND THEN THREE, AND THEN TEN
AND I CAN'T SEEM TO GET YOU OUT OF MY HEAD
I'M TRAPPED INSIDE YOUR HOUSE OF GINGERBREAD.

WHERE YOU SPUN ME AROUND
IN THE COLD, CRISPY NIGHT
ON THAT DECK BACK IN DENVER
GOD, THAT LOOK IN YOUR EYE
JUST LIKE CHRISTMAS.

I SWEAR, THAT NIGHT FELT LIKE CHRISTMAS
IN YOUR ARMS, JUST LIKE CHRISTMAS
MY HANDS IN YOUR HAIR, JUST LIKE CHRISTMAS
THE WAY YOU WOULD STARE, CALL ME CHRISTMAS

I WAS THERE, YOU WERE THERE, WE WERE THERE

*(Big piano, instrumental finish. Then –)*

(*A shift.*)

**MARGOT.**  I don't know you.

**GRACIE.**  No, you don't.

**MARGOT.**  But I feel like I know you...or that I should.

**GRACIE.**  In a way, you kind of do.

**MARGOT.**  How?

**GRACIE.**  I died *way* before you were born but just because we never met, doesn't mean I wasn't always there.

> (**GRACIE** *smirks.* **MARGOT** *takes this in, still can't place her.*)

**MARGOT.**  I'm so sorry, I'm drawing a blank here.

**GRACIE.**  That's okay. We're not here to talk about the past, we're here to talk about the present! And the future. And the past too, I guess. Whatever, I'm an Aquarius, okay?!

**MARGOT.**  What's your name?

**GRACIE.**  Gracie.

**MARGOT.**  Gracie... Gracie...

**GRACIE.**  No one comes to mind? Really?

**MARGOT.**  Honestly, no. Tonight's been a series of unexpected visitors, each one stranger than the one before and you, Gracie, as of right now, are by *far* the strangest.

**GRACIE.**  Ha! You sound like your mom.

**MARGOT.**  You knew my mom?

> (*Beat.*)

**GRACIE.**  (*Smiling big.*) How about I read you a story?

**MARGOT.**  I don't have time for stories –

*(Too late. **GRACIE** pulls out a picture book from beneath the counter. She holds it on her lap as if she were leading "story time" with the audience, flipping pages as she reads.)*

*(The illustrations on the book should either be hilarious like stick figures and poorly drawn landscapes, or elaborate and lush as if it were professionally published.)*

**GRACIE.**  Once upon a time, there was a little boy named Gustavo.

*(She turns the page of the story book.)*

**MARGOT.**  Gracie, I'm really exhausted from all these possessions, and I –

**GRACIE.**  He grew up in a little town in a far away land. It was a town called, "Phoenix."

*(She turns the page.)*

And the little boy grew up in this town called Phoenix feeling really sad, really alone, and really, *really* creative. Aw.

*(**GRACIE** smirks. She turns the page.)*

Gustavo had a cousin. A feisty little girl. Her name was Dolores.

*(She waits to turn the page. **MARGOT** perks up.)*

**MARGOT.**  Dolores?

**GRACIE.**  Yes. Dolores.

*(Beat.)*

Might you know someone named Dolores?

*(Beat.)*

**MARGOT**.  I might.

**GRACIE**.  Is there anything you wanna share about her?

**MARGOT**.  Other than she was my mother? No.

*(Beat.)*

But you already knew that.

*(**GRACIE** gives a small, sympathetic smile. Then – she turns the page.)*

**GRACIE**.  Whenever Gustavo's mom was at work or hanging out with her friends at the casino, his older cousin, Dolores, would come over and take care of him. And together, they would try on his mom's dresses and her makeup and Dolores would look at Gustavo in the mirror and say, "Wow! Gorgeous! <u>Radiant</u>!" And she would say, "I love you, Gustavo."

*(She turns the page.)*

And Gustavo would look at her, his lipstick all smeared and clumsy and would say, "When we're together, can you call me Gracie instead?" And Dolores smiled, and nodded and said, "Of course. Gracie. That's a beautiful name." Dolores loved Gracie so very much. And Gracie loved Dolores.

*(She turns the page.)*

Then one day, Gracie's mom came home from work early to find the two of them playing with her makeup and dresses and she got <u>so angry</u>, she grabbed Gustavo's things, threw them out of the house, and told him to never, <u>ever</u> come back again. And Gustavo cried. A lot. All night, really.

*(She turns the page.)*

**GRACIE**.  But Dolores wasn't having any of it. She marched right up to Gracie's mom, her Tía, and said, "You don't want him here? Fine. He's coming with me." And just like that, Gustavo (and Gracie) went to live with Dolores for the rest of his life.

Or at least until he turned eighteen.

*(She turns the page.)*

Dolores and Gracie grew up together. And Gracie started wearing Dolores' clothes not just at home, but wherever she went. Gustavo became a ghost of Christmas past, and Gracie became the joy of Christmas present. And Gracie *loved* performing. It was her happy place. She wrote songs, and sang them...and Dolores was her biggest fan.

*(She turns the page.)*

Then one day, Gracie knew she had to leave the nest if she wanted to be a singer, so she made her way east to the Big Apple where dreams come true. And she had a wild, incredible time there. Lots of men. <u>Lots</u> of men.

*(She giggles, turns the page.)*

Then one night at a house party, after performing for a few friends in the basement of some bar in Bed-Stuy, she went to the roof to look at the full moon. She loved the moon, Gracie did. It called to her. It pulled her. She always fell into a trance, looking at it. And as she stood on the roof of that bar, taking a step closer towards the moon's gorgeous light... Gracie took a step too far...and she fell.

*(Sudden; animated.)* SPLAT!

**(GRACIE** *laughs, turns the page.)*

The! End!

(**GRACIE** *slams the book shut.*)

Moral of the story, kids? Never...*ever*...wear wedges on a rooftop bar in Brooklyn while under the influence of drugs, alcohol, or both at the same time.

**MARGOT.** That's horrible!

**GRACIE.** Accidents happen. <u>So</u>! Do you remember me now...?

**MARGOT.** I do. There was a picture of you and my mom on our fridge when y'all were kids. She talked about you a lot. Mostly about how much she missed you and your music.

**GRACIE.** She was my biggest fan, my prima Dolores.

**MARGOT.** Yeah. She was mine too.

(*Beat. A moment. Then:*)

**GRACIE.** How are you feeling right now, Margot?

**MARGOT.** I dunno.

**GRACIE.** Think.

**MARGOT.** I don't know what you want me to say.

**GRACIE.** All night, you've had the craziest of the crazies visit you during your night shift before Christmas, coming in and out of this –

(*She takes in her surroundings.*)

Where are we?

**MARGOT.** (*Less mad, more sad.*) Happy Burger.

**GRACIE.** Right. Happy Burger.

(*She's not even gonna ask.*)

And still nothing? You can't tap into what your heart might be feeling? Not even a little bit?

> (**MARGOT**'s *eyes look over to the blue cardigan on the plastic chair, only for a quick beat. Then:*)

**MARGOT.** I think we're done here.

**GRACIE.** But we're just getting started.

**MARGOT.** *You* might be getting started, but I've been here all night, so. I really think you should go.

**GRACIE.** Not until you stop avoiding the pain buried deep inside you.

**MARGOT.** I don't want to.

**GRACIE.** But you *have* to.

**MARGOT.** Why? Why do I have to? Why do I have to sit with something that doesn't make me feel good? That makes me feel like shit? That makes me want to throw up every time I feel it?

**GRACIE.** Throwing up is good for you, actually.

**MARGOT.** How is that good?!

**GRACIE.** So you get it all out! So you don't keep things bottled up like a Mexican Coke that's ready to explode.

**MARGOT.** Are you done? I really need to pee and I *don't* need an audience for that.

**GRACIE.** You and I both know you don't have to pee. But sure, that's okay, I can leave now.

> (*She starts to leave, then suddenly stops herself.*)

Oh! And to be clear? In case you hadn't caught on? I'm not the person who's coming for you, Margot. There's one more spirit waiting to be let in. Just one more.

> (*Beat.*)

But you know that. Don't you.

*(**GRACIE** puts the piano keyboard away, starts walking towards the door.)*

When she comes, tell her thanks for me, please. Tell her I said thanks for giving me the concert I've always dreamed of.

*(And just like that, **GRACIE** disappears in a burst of light back to the spirit realm, leaving **MARGOT** in this Happy Burger – alone.)*

*(Beat. A moment. Then –)*

*(**MARGOT** thrashes in a fit of rage. Everything she's been holding in all night she releases here and now. She throws Christmas ornaments, kicks the boxes of Secret Happy Sauce, screams and yells – it's animalistic.)*

*(She's about to throw the carafe of Happy Burger coffee but then – the logo catches her eye and she stops.)*

*(Beat. A moment.)*

*(Silence and emptiness start to sink in. The Happy Burger feels more hollow than when we first started. Then –)*

*(**MARGOT** walks over to the blue cardigan that's been haunting her this entire time. She grabs it, smells it, and puts it on. Then:)*

**MARGOT.**  *(Relinquishes.)* Okay. You can come in now.

*(Suddenly, the presence of a spirit or entity of some kind floats throughout the space as counters rumble and fryer oil boils – the first time a spirit has made itself physically known before jumping into **MARGOT**'s body.)*

*(This spiritual entity is concealed – scarier than it actually is. But like most things in the shadows, they stay shrouded in darkness until exposed to the light. Silence. Then –)*

**MARGOT.** *(Singing.)*
NOCHE DE PAZ, NOCHE DE AMOR
TODO DUERME, EN DERREDOR
DESDE LOS ASTROS QUE ESPARCEN SU LUZ
BELLA ANUNCIANDO AL NIÑITO JESÚS
BRILLA LA ESTRELLA DE PAZ.
BRILLA LA ESTRELLA DE PAZ.

*(As she sings, **MARGOT** slowly becomes possessed. This possession isn't like the others. It's gradual. Seamless. The end of the song isn't sung by **MARGOT**...but is sung by her mother. She looks around as she sings.)*

*(As **DOLORES**: mid-fifties. A kind, compassionate soul with a smile that could light up any room. Her energy is pure – something that feels untouched. Something that heals all wounds. An ancestral maternal spiritual entity. The type of mother you forgot you needed.)*

*(**DOLORES** takes it all in. In shock that she's actually here right now. A moment, then –)*

*(Excited. Fierce. Young at heart.)*

**DOLORES.** It worked? It actually worked! Ha!

*(She laughs.)*

Oh my goodness, I can't believe I'm here.

*(She touches everything she can.)*

I'm touching things, I'm really *touching* things! Guao. This place hasn't changed one bit.

*(To* **MARGOT**.*)* Do you know how many times I've tried reaching you? Hijuesu!

I'm just glad these spirits were the right combination that would guide me to you, Margarita. Which makes sense, I mean who else was gonna tell you how to get your life right other than a chola, a gambler, my musically inclined cousin, and tu madre of course! I had an ask out to Selena but she's very busy.

*(She walks over to an empty Happy Burger table.)*

Can I sit here?

*(Beat. A moment.)*

*(***MARGOT**, *as herself, nods her head.)*

*(Then, as if the table were made of glass itself,* **DOLORES** *slowly takes a seat and closes her eyes.)*

*(She gently soothes the table with the palm of her hand like it were a child.)*

I don't know why I've always loved this table. Something about it just...makes me Happy.

*(Beat. A moment. A shift in* **MARGOT**. *Overwhelmed by this feeling, this presence...)*

**MARGOT**. Mom?

*(***DOLORES** *nods her head.)*

Oh my god...

*(Beat. A moment.)*

**DOLORES**. Don't be scared, *mijita*.

**MARGOT**. I'm not scared, I'm...

*(She can't name this feeling. So instead:)*

**MARGOT.**  You feel like light inside of me.

**DOLORES.**  That's not my light. It's yours. And it's a light I've felt ever since you were born.

*(Beat. A moment.)*

The day I brought you home from the hospital, I was terrified. I walked into our tiny little apartment, no one else but you and me, ready to take on the world together. And I remember thinking to myself, "how do I keep this beautiful, little thing alive?" Because that was my one job. To keep you alive.

*(Beat.)*

And also to not go to jail. Seriously. I had nightmares about it. That one day the police would come and see me put whiskey on your gums while you were teething and they'd call CPS and I'd go to jail. Or you'd fall off the roof from putting up our Christmas lights and they'd bring me in for questioning and then put me in jail. Or you'd get pulled over from driving my drunk ass home from your cousin Letty's Christmas party and the cops would blame me because I was all peda and never put you on my insurance, which would what? *Land me in jail*.

*(Serious now:)*

My whole life, my biggest fear was losing you, or not being able to be there for you when you needed me the most. And for the three years the sickness took over, I had to live with that fear becoming my reality. Trying to make peace with it in whatever way I could.

*(**MARGOT** pulls out a souvenir Christmas-themed Happy Burger Coffee Tumbler from her bag. Maybe these same tumblers are sold at the concessions stand for drinks.)*

**MARGOT.**  I bought this for you. You always wanted one and I always told you they were too expensive. But I bought you one the last time I went to grab you a Happy Burger Coffee because I wanted to surprise you. To make you Happy.

**DOLORES.**  *(Remembering.)* I loved that Happy Burger Coffee. Black. You brought me that coffee every morning. Five a.m. till the day I died. I'll never forget that.

*(Then:)*

It was Lupe's speciality, you know.

Everyone always thought it was Raúl who made the coffee but that man, sweet as he is, couldn't operate a Keurig let alone brew homemade coffee for hundreds of customers.

*(Then:)*

Another lesson for you, mija: behind every man holding a delicious cup of coffee, is the woman who got him up at five in the morning and brewed it for him.

**MARGOT.**  The day you died... I didn't get back to the hospital in time to give you your coffee. You were already gone.

*(Beat. A moment. Then:)*

How could you leave me without saying goodbye?

*(Beat.)*

**DOLORES.**  *(Tough Mexican mom.)* Let me tell you something, mijita. Sit down, get comfortable.

*(She does.)*

I started keeping a journal while I was in the hospital.

**MARGOT.**  *(This is new info.)* You kept a journal?

**DOLORES**. Oh yeah. I wrote down my thoughts, prayers, poetry, dreams... Even the salacious ones. I had a dream once with John Stamos where we were in the back seat of his car, and we, uh –

**MARGOT**. Yeah, I don't need to hear all that.

**DOLORES**. Hm. Your loss. Anyway. On the last page of that journal, I wrote you a letter. *That's* where I left your goodbye. The hospital packed all my things in a little box for you to take home, but you never went to pick it up.

I even left something for you to give my sister, your Tía Rosalie... *(Mexican mom guilt.)* But I guess she'll never receive it...

*(Skillfully played.)* It's okay though. I paid her a visit on my way over here to check in on her. She never sees me, but she knows I'm there. Watching. Listening. Judging her like I used to.

*(Beat. Majorly judgmental –)*

Did you know that mujer moved in with your cousin Letty?

**MARGOT**. No. I didn't know. Letty never tells me anything anymore.

**DOLORES**. Well maybe if you'd pay her a visit every now and then, she might tell you a thing or two.

*(Beat. A moment. Then:)*

Yeah so your Tía Rosalie moved in with tu cousin Letty. She wanted to be "closer to family," o ya se que, especially after I died. The sentiment is nice pero que pedo. Why would she do that to herself, there's no parking over there.

*(Beat, then:)*

She looks good, though. Her hair is as long as the branches of a willow tree, with grey streaks thick and proud like a skunk. The stress of living with her needy daughter has made her look older than she is, but her laugh is exactly as I remember it. Like a witch.

*(She laughs.)*

The other night, I watched her take shrooms and around hour three, she was wandering around Letty's succulent garden out back. It was so funny, the way she'd whisper things to the Bunny Ear Cactus so someone out there can keep her secrets.

*(As Tía Rosalie, whispering.)* "Hello little cactus. I'm not afraid to die. But I'm afraid everyone around me will."

*(Beat. A moment. Then:)*

I miss that mujer. My dear, sweet sister. Almost as much as I miss you.

*(**MARGOT** nods. Beat. A moment. Then:)*

**MARGOT.** I'm sorry I didn't go back for your things, Mom. I'd give anything to have your letter right about now.

**DOLORES.** Oh stop being so dramatic, I have your letter right here.

*(She pulls out a folded letter.)*

What? I'm a spirit! I have my ways.

*(**DOLORES** clears her throat.)*

*(Reading, big smile:)* "My dearest Margarita, it's me. Your mom. If you're reading this, that means I'm dead. And there are a few things I need you to know since I won't be there to tell you myself. But I don't even know where to start! Let's see…

*(She thinks; then:)*

**DOLORES.** Ah! Always have a pair of slip-on shoes in case you don't feel like bending over to tie them before you leave the house. That's a good one, right? What else...

*(She thinks; then:)*

Oh! Don't forget...to make the time...to get laid. I know you don't wanna hear that from *me* but what's life without a little fun?! Hm... What else, what else...

*(She thinks; then:)*

OH! This one's *very* important. I used to tell you this a lot when you were little, te acuerdas? Aver. Always plan ahead. Because when you plan *ahead*, you'll always have food, you won't go to jail, and you won't lose your car in the middle of Vegas, don't ask.

*(Re: her advice.)* I think this is a good start.

*(The final stretch.)* Now, be sure to take good care of yourself, eh? Call your cousin Letty, la tonta. Pobresita, your Tía Rosalie dropped her on her head when she was a baby so don't be mad at her for her lack of social skills and awkward exchanges, okay?

*(Not wanting this to end.)* Is there anything else I missed, let's see...

*(She thinks; then:)*

Don't forget to eat. And drink forty-eight ounces of water every single day. Never forget where you came from either, okay? Remember your roots, they keep you sturdy. And strong. Like a tree. Even during a hurricane.

*(The end.)* Anyway. That's all I wanted to say. Love, Mom."

> *(She folds the letter closed, puts it away.* **MARGOT** *takes this in. Then:)*

**MARGOT**.  Mom, this letter is lovely, it is, but it doesn't make me feel any better. In fact, I feel worse.

**DOLORES**.  I know Christmas time is hard for you, mija. If I lost *you* on Christmas Eve, it would be hard for me, too. So I get why you don't want to leave this place. It was our mother daughter lunch spot. And we loved a good burger. With Texas Twirls. <u>And</u> Onion Thrills. Medium. With an ice cold Dr. Pepper to finish it all off. But my spirit isn't connected to Happy Burger querida. It isn't tied to these cheaply designed smiley faces and ugly old chairs. My spirit is connected to *you*. So it's time, *mi vida*. It's time you let this place go. It's time you let *me* go.

**MARGOT**.  I don't wanna forget you. Your laugh, your smile, the sound of your voice...

**DOLORES**.  But you *will* forget those things, Margarita. And that's okay. Because what you *won't* forget? What will stay with you forever? Is my spirit.

And *that's* worth holding on to.

>    (**MARGOT** *rubs her chest.*)

**MARGOT**.  I feel my heart growing and breaking at the same time.

**DOLORES**.  Not just your heart. Mine too.

>    (*Beat. A moment.*)

I will always be with you, amorcita. Wherever you go... I won't be too far.

>    (*Beat. A moment.*)

>    (*Then, a small hiccup escapes* **MARGOT***'s lips. And just like that,* **DOLORES** *is gone.*)

>    (*The lights from the restaurant slowly rise back to when we first started.*)

**MARGOT.**  Mom? Mom, you still there?

*(Beat. A moment. Then:)*

**ROBOTIC SANTA.**  *"It's me! Santa! Bringing your favorite dose of Holiday Cheer!"*

*(**MARGOT** slowly turns towards **SANTA**.)*

*(She takes him in. Could this be...)*

**MARGOT.**  Oh my god...

*(She takes a step towards him, slowly walking towards him as he does his little dance.)*

It can't be...

Can it?

*(She holds him up.)*

*(Turns him around.)*

*(And opens the compartment where his batteries should be.)*

*(But instead –)*

*(To **SANTA**.)* There's nothing. What happened to your batteries, Grumpy Santa?

*(There are no batteries inside and there weren't any to begin with...)*

*(Beat. Then:)*

**ROBOTIC SANTA.**  *"I quit! Get your own free stuff!"*

*(**MARGOT** screams. **SANTA** now sounds a lot like her mother...)*

*(Half **SANTA** voice, half **DOLORES**:)*

*"I'm always <u>watchin' you</u>... Always!"*

> *(The sound of the "ding" from the drive-thru window.* **MARGOT** *turns towards the drive thru, the beaming headlights telling her that there's a real car out there this time, with a real person, waiting to have their order taken.)*

**RAÚL**. *(Voice-over.)* Howdy! Hola! Bonjour! Welcome to Happy Burger! This is Raúl speaking, founder and President of Joy, bringing you Crispy Cheer with every bite since 1979. Hang tight – someone will be with you shortly. Ciao!

> *(As Raúl's message comes through,* **MARGOT** *takes in the Happy Burger before her – in all its disarray. The entire night she just experienced.)*

> *(Honk! Honk Honk!)*

> *(***MARGOT*** *puts* **SANTA** *back in his place, makes her way back behind the counter, puts on the headset. Something about her has changed.)*

**MARGOT**.  Hi there. Welcome to Happy Burger, proud home of the Happy Burger, would you like to try our Happy Burger Happy –

> *(She stops herself. A moment. Then:)*

Sorry, yes I'm still here.

Um. Yeah, I'm so sorry but um...

...

...

We're closed.

Merry Christmas.

> *(She takes off her headset and puts it down.)*

*(Throughout the following, we hear angry mumbles coming from the customer through the headset, and the sound of a car honking incessantly until it eventually fades away.)*

*(Then, **MARGOT** starts closing up shop – she turns off the grills, the fryers, the lights, everything.)*

*(Then –)*

*(**MARGOT** pulls out her cell phone, dials.)*

MARGOT.  *(On the phone.)* Hey Raúl, hey. It's me. Merry Christmas to you too. Yes, everything's fine. It's...great, actually. Listen, I'm sorry to do this on Christmas Eve but um...

*(Beat. A moment. Then:)*

*(On the phone.)* I quit. I can't thank you enough for everything you and your family did for me, Raúl. Especially this last year... I will never forget it.

*(Beat. A moment.)*

*(A slight look of panic on **MARGOT**'s face. She didn't quite think this whole thing through!)*

*(On the phone.)* Um. I <u>don't</u> have a key but...you know what? I'll just turn off all the lights and everything should be safe and sound for the night, don't you think? What, I can't hear you! *Cshhh!* You're breaking up! *Cshh, csshh! CSHHHHH!*

*(She hangs up the phone. Looks around for a bit.)*

*(She unplugs all the Christmas light decor from around the restaurant until only the lights from the small Christmas tree can be seen.)*

*(And the luminarias that have been dark this whole time slowly come to life. The light of candles burning inside brown paper bags look like little stars among us.)*

*(**MARGOT** looks around, surveying the damage left in the wake of every single night visit. Something outside catches her eye.)*

...It's still snowing. Wow...

*(She pulls out her phone from her pocket as she heads towards the door. Stuck to her phone...is **CLYDE**'s hundred dollar bill. She knows what she has to do...)*

*(She dials the phone. It rings for a moment. Someone answers.)*

*(On the phone.)* Hey Letty. It's me, Margarita. Can I still come over?

*(Something outside catches her eye.)*

*(On the phone.)* Oh, hold on a sec.

*(As she heads out the door –)*

*(Waving the cash.)* Hey Rico! RICO! I got somethin' for ya!

*(And just like that, she's gone.)*

*(Then, **SANTA** comes back to life – dances a little dance. Bah Humbug!)*

*(Black.)*

**End of Play**

www.ingramcontent.com/pod-product-compliance
Lightning Source LLC
Chambersburg PA
CBHW070416120726
47909CB00005B/1678

* 9 7 8 0 5 7 3 7 1 1 9 6 1 *